# DRAGON STORM

## Kai and Boneshadow

Also in the series:

TOMAS AND IRONSKIN

CARA AND SILVERTHIEF

ELLIS AND PATHSEEKER

MIRA AND FLAMETELLER


Coming soon:

ERIN AND ROCKHAMMER

CONNOR AND LIGHTSPIRIT

SKYE AND SOULSINGER

# DRAGON STORM

## Kai and Boneshadow

### ALASTAIR CHISHOLM

nosy
crow

First published in the UK in 2022 by Nosy Crow Ltd
The Crow's Nest, 14 Baden Place,
Crosby Row, London, SE1 1YW, UK

Nosy Crow Eireann Ltd
44 Orchard Grove, Kenmare,
Co Kerry, V93 FY22, Ireland

Nosy Crow and associated logos are trademarks
and/or registered trademarks of Nosy Crow Ltd

Text © Alastair Chisholm, 2022
Cover illustration © Ben Mantle, 2022
Inside illustrations © Eric Deschamps, 2022

The right of Alastair Chisholm, Ben Mantle, and Eric Deschamps to be
identified as the author and illustrators of this work has been asserted.

ISBN: 978 1 83994 224 2

A CIP catalogue record for this book is available from the British Library

Printed and bound in Great Britain by Clays Ltd, Elcograf S.p.A.

Papers used by Nosy Crow are made from wood grown in sustainable forests.

1 3 5 7 9 10 8 6 4 2

www.nosycrow.com

# IN THE LAND OF DRACONIS, THERE ARE NO DRAGONS.

Once, there were. Once, humans
and dragons were friends, and guarded
the land. They were wise, and strong, and
created the great city of Rivven together.

But then came the Dragon Storm, and
the dragons retreated from the world
of humans. To the men and women of
Draconis, they became legends and myth.

And so, these days, in the land of Draconis,
there are no dragons…

…Or so people thought.

# KAI

Under the heart of Rivven was a cave. Hardly anyone in the city knew it existed, and even fewer knew how to find it, and yet it was huge – a cavern so vast that you could hardly see from one end to the other. Soft glowing lamps hung from its roof like tiny suns, shining down on a world that was a home, a training ground, a school, and a place of secrets.

It was the Dragonseer Guild Hall ... and

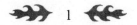

today it was a racecourse.

"Come on, Boneshadow!" called Kai as they hurtled around the track. "You're doing great!"

He glanced back as they reached the second bend. Behind him was Erin, then Tom and Connor almost neck and neck, then the others. Kai was leading, but

they were only halfway round.

"How are you feeling?" he called down.

Beneath him, Boneshadow laughed. "Wonderful!" she cried.

Kai tucked his head down and grinned. He was in a saddle and his feet were secure in stirrups, but it wasn't a horse he was riding. This creature's skin was smooth and dry, and as white as bone. She had a long neck, and a large head, and on her chest was a red flare, and Kai sat tucked between two folded wings.

She was Boneshadow, and she was a *dragon*.

"Rockhammer's close behind us!" Kai called. Behind him, Erin's dragon,

Rockhammer, was huge and fierce looking, with great spikes, and the ground shuddered with every stride. Erin's face had a look of grim determination.

"He'll get tired," called back Boneshadow. "Hold on!"

They raced around the curve. Kai could feel Boneshadow's powerful muscles move, and could sense her thoughts, too – the beat of her heart, the joy of running, the feeling that she could keep going forever. He could feel all this because, like the other children, he was a *dragonseer*. Boneshadow was his dragon, and he was her human.

They straightened out, and Boneshadow stretched her legs. The air whistled through

# Kai and Boneshadow

Kai's short black hair and made his brown eyes water, and he blinked and laughed. The ground shuddered, and he realised that Rockhammer was catching up with them. The big dragon was faster on the straight, where his long legs could eat up the distance. Ahead of them was the next fence. Boneshadow adjusted her pace.

"Ready?" she growled. Kai held on tight, and the dragon bunched her hind legs and *leapt* over the fence, landing with hardly a jolt. On her back, the white leathery wings stayed folded – like many dragons, Boneshadow could fly, but this was a running race only. Kai felt the *thump* behind him as Rockhammer leapt and cleared the fence too. He could hear Erin bellowing and knew they were right behind – but already the next bend was coming up, and Boneshadow, more nimble, leaned tight into the curve and pulled away again.

Rockhammer caught them on the third straight, coming up to the last corner. He was tired, Kai could tell, and his big pink tongue flopped around in his mouth like a dog's. Twenty metres to go, and Boneshadow was just ahead. If they could make the corner, Kai knew she had the energy for the final sprint!

Erin shouted something into Rockhammer's ear and the big dragon nodded. He started to drift sideways, into

Boneshadow's line. Kai glanced at him in alarm.

"Hey!" he yelped.

Ten metres to the bend and the big dragon was very close, almost brushing against them. Five metres...

"Whoa!" called Kai suddenly, and dragged on the reins. Boneshadow eased up immediately, and with a whoop Erin and Rockhammer took the racing line and pulled ahead around the corner. Now they were in the lead, and Boneshadow had lost her pace; she accelerated as they came into the final straight, and almost caught up, but Rockhammer stretched out his long neck and crossed the finish line first.

# DRAGON STORM

"YASSSSSS!" shouted Erin. Rockhammer gave a huge bellow.

Behind them, Kai and Boneshadow eased to a halt. Kai slid down from the dragon's back and patted her.

"Sorry, Bone," he said with a rueful smile. "If we'd gone for the turn, we would have collided with Rockhammer."

Boneshadow shook her large white head. "We were ahead of them," she said softly. "They should have given way for us."

"I know," said Kai. "But I didn't want to take the risk. Anyway, the race was fun even if we didn't win, right?"

Boneshadow chuckled and rested her head against Kai's shoulder. "Of course," she said.

# Kai and Boneshadow

"But I'm not sure Vice Chancellor Creedy agrees..."

Kai looked up. Striding towards them were two of the senior Guild members. Vice Chancellor Creedy was dressed all in grey and his face was drawn into a dour scowl. Beside him was Daisy, who taught self-defence. She walked with a bouncing happy stride, in bright-yellow leggings that seemed to glow in comparison to Creedy's dull robes.

"Boy!" snapped Creedy, pointing at Kai. "What was that?"

Kai blinked. "Um... Well, sir, I didn't want—"

"You pulled up," said Creedy. "You had the racing line and you pulled up!" He scowled.

"This isn't a *game*, you know. The purpose of these races is to learn how to deal with high-pressure situations. Do you think, when real danger arises, that being *nice* will help? Hmm?"

Kai shook his head. "No, sir."

"No, sir," repeated Creedy. "I despair."

Beside him, Daisy grinned. "Oh, it wasn't so bad. That was some good racing, Kai! And, Boneshadow, you took those corners well." She nodded her head towards Creedy and gave a tiny wink, making Kai grin. Creedy sighed.

"Och, away," he said irritably, waving a hand. "That's enough for today. Put away your harnesses – *tidily* now!"

Kai and Boneshadow headed back to the training ground. Ahead of them, Erin was doing a victory dance and Rockhammer was walking in a great swagger, his huge mouth open and grinning.

"It *was* a good race," said Boneshadow as they headed back.

"Yeah," said Kai.

*Would have been good to win though,* he thought.

# DINNER

Kai carefully folded up Boneshadow's harness and packed it in one of the chests by the training ground. Erin had left hers sloppy and undone, and Kai tidied that away as well, before wandering back to the dining hut with Tom, his best friend.

"Good race!" said Tom. He'd come third on his dragon, Ironskin. Tom was taller and bigger than Kai; he was a blacksmith's son, wide-shouldered and strong, where Kai was slim. Ironskin was tall and broad too, and her skin was a deep dark red, with bright lines like fire in a forge. She and Tom were alike in personality – both were loyal and protective.

"Did Creedy give you a hard time?" asked Tom.

Kai shrugged. He didn't really let it bother him. Some people got worked up about things, but Kai was always able to let them wash over him. "No, he was fine."

Tom laughed and shook his head. "You're too nice, Kai," he said.

Kai smiled. "Funny, that's what he said too."

They reached the hut, and Kai turned

to Boneshadow. "See you later," he said. Boneshadow nodded. And then, as Kai watched, she faded away until she was completely gone. Beside her, Ironskin did the same.

The dragons were from a different world, a world that was hard to imagine. Drun, who taught summoning, called it a world of *ideas*. "Every dragon is different," he'd say. "They each got their own shape, their own way of bein'. You're dragonseers, and that means you all got the power to reach into their world and make a connection. And if they want, they can come across. And when they do, their shape, the way they are ... comes from *you*."

# Kai and Boneshadow

Kai could still feel the faint whisper of that connection in his mind, and he smiled. He and Tom entered the hut and sat down for dinner just as Hilda, the cook, was serving up. This evening it was a rich potato pie, perfect after a day of exercise, and the children tucked in, chattering.

There was Cara, pale and thin, sitting very still as she liked to do. Cara often kept to herself, but today she was looking at a map of Ellis's. Ellis was showing her routes, drawing them carefully with a pencil. Then Mira, short but bustling with energy, her long black hair tied back and smears of oil on her face as usual, for Mira loved tinkering with machinery. Connor was reading a book at the table, his curly hair hanging over his face like a curtain, and Erin sat at the head of the table, looking pleased with herself and telling everyone again how she'd won the race. Tom grinned at Kai and rolled his eyes, but Kai didn't mind.

"Oh, enough!" grumbled Connor at last.

# Kai and Boneshadow

Erin was tall and athletic, while Connor far preferred reading his books, and the two of them often squabbled.

"Oh, sorry," said Erin. "I thought maybe you couldn't see the rest of the race, being so far at the back!" She gave a loud booming laugh and Connor bristled.

"It's summoning practice tomorrow," he

said. "Not that *most* of us need practice..."

Erin scowled. She'd been in the Guild for longer than any of the others, but she couldn't get the hang of summoning Rockhammer, her dragon, and needed help every time.

"It was a good race," said Kai, stepping in before they started arguing. "Well done, Erin. Rockhammer was brilliant."

Erin, still cross, made an effort to smile. "Thank you," she said. "Boneshadow did well too." Then she brightened. "Hey, did I ever tell you all how I met Rocky?"

"Only about twenty times," muttered Connor, but Erin ignored him and told her story, while Kai patiently listened. Erin liked telling the story – it always cheered her up – and Kai didn't mind hearing it again.

"... and then this huge boulder crashed down on to the house!" said Erin.

Sometimes she exaggerated, and sometimes the details changed. Kai wondered if there was another story she wasn't telling. But he kept nodding and smiling.

"... and when I saw who'd rescued us ... it was Rockhammer!" finished Erin. She grinned around the table. "What about you, Kai? How did you meet Boneshadow?"

Kai smiled. He could feel the dragon's presence in his mind, listening in. She liked the story as much as he did.

"In a book," he said.

"A book?" asked Mira, frowning.

Kai nodded. "My mum looks after animals. She treats them, and studies them. She knows *so much* about them! And she's got all these books on anatomy, and bone structure, and things like that. She collects books wherever she goes."

Connor looked interested, despite himself.

"Some of the books are ancient," said Kai. "They've got pictures of animals that don't even exist – gryphons, basilisks ... and *dragons*. She showed me the pictures, and there was one, looking out of the page, and, I don't know, there was just something about its eyes..."

# Kai and Boneshadow

He shook his head, remembering. "I couldn't sleep that night. It was like the book was calling to me. I got out of bed, crept downstairs... I could see the book on the shelf and it seemed to be *glowing*."

He remembered the feel of the old paper, crackling as he turned the pages, and there it was, the drawing, in faded old ink – a strange white creature with a red flare across her chest. Her mouth was open and sharp teeth showed, but her eyes seemed friendly. She was staring at Kai, and somehow, even though it was impossible, Kai had known she could see him. He'd reached out and stroked a finger down the line of her back, and stared in astonishment as the drawing stretched its neck, as pale as bone, and blew a tiny puff of breath like a shadow across the page.

*Hmm*, a voice had said – not out loud, but inside his head, like a dream. *Bone ... shadow. Yesssssss...*

"I knew right then," said Kai. "I knew she was my dragon."

*And you were my human*, said Boneshadow.

Erin sniffed. "That's nice." She sounded bored. "Mine was more exciting."

"Of course," said Kai, smiling.

It was the boys' turn to clear up after dinner, and the four of them – Ellis, Tom, Connor and Kai – were on their way back to their

# Kai and Boneshadow

dorm when they heard a horn blowing from the centre of the Hall, long and clear.

"That's the Gathering Call," said Connor, surprised. "What's going on?"

They turned back towards the main buildings. Kai reached out in his mind

and called Boneshadow, and she appeared beside him. She stretched her neck and sniffed.

"What's happening?" she asked.

"No idea."

They gathered in front of Berin's office. Berin stood, waiting, with Malik.

Berin was the Chancellor of the Dragonseer Guild. Tall and graceful, with dark skin and white hair, she wore a light-blue robe and carried a staff. She smiled as they arrived. Beside her, Malik was dressed in black, with curling black hair. Officially, Malik was one of the King's Clerks, managing the paperwork needed to run the kingdom. But secretly he was a member of the Dragonseer Guild. He looked worried.

Kai glanced around as they arrived. Everyone else was there – the other children, Creedy and Daisy, Drun and Hilda. The children had all summoned their dragons, except for Erin. Connor's dragon Lightspirit was a thin, twisting creature, almost snake-like. Ironskin loomed over Tom, while Pathseeker, Ellis's dragon, stood shoulder to shoulder with Ellis. Mira's strange Flameteller, with his bronze colouring and straight features, stood like a clockwork toy, and beside him were Cara and Silverthief, whose shifting colours seemed to blend into the background. They waited, curious.

# DRAGON STORM

"We're sorry to disturb your evening," said Berin, "but a situation has arisen." She nodded to Malik, and he stepped forward.

"Dragonseers," he called. "You have all been summoned to the Royal Palace ... *by order of the king.*"

# THE
# PALACE

Kai and the others stared at Malik, and there was a buzz of worried chatter. Malik held up one hand.

"Let me explain. You may be aware of a trade negotiation taking place just now?"

"The Southern Cities," said Connor.

Malik nodded. "Exactly. The kingdom of Draconis is negotiating a new treaty with the city nations of Borolo and Venn. The King's Clerks have been working hard: preparing

agreements, making copies, revising and so on. We're almost finished, and the Clerks' division went for a celebration dinner. But..." He shook his head. "It seems there was a bad batch of mutton served at the meal, and they've been struck down with food poisoning. *All* of them, nearly." He looked irritated.

"There's no one to complete the work. Prince Harald has been leading the negotiations, and he suggested—" Malik hesitated. "He suggested we should use the apprentice clerks."

It took Kai a few moments to realise what Malik meant, and then he turned to Tom in shock. Tom stared back, amazed.

# Kai and Boneshadow

Kai and his friends were dragonseers, chosen and brought to the Guild because they had a unique power: to open a path to the world of dragons, and invite a dragon into their world. But the rest of Rivven didn't know that. They thought dragons were a myth – tales to frighten small children, of horrible fierce creatures who hunted humans.

And so, to the outside world, and even to most of the children's parents, there was a different story. Officially, the children were *apprentice clerks*, learning a trade to help them through their lives.

And now Prince Harald wanted his apprentice clerks to turn up for work.

"But we can't do that," said Erin, looking alarmed. "I mean, we're not *real* clerks!"

"Certainly not you," muttered Connor. "Can you even read?"

"Shut up!" she snapped, but Berin held up a hand.

"Calm yourselves." Her voice was confident and soothing, and Erin, glaring at Connor, fell silent. Berin smiled at them all. "This is an odd situation, but you *have* been learning your clerk skills. You can all read and write well, you can tally tables and create contracts. No one expects you to be experts – Prince Harald just needs you to finish copying some documents. Malik will come with you and look after you all. Think of it as a rather unusual adventure." She beamed.

"Now. You'll set off first thing, so take this evening to pack what you need, make sure your clerks' uniforms are clean and get an early night. Tomorrow you will meet the prince."

She nodded to them, and they were dismissed.

"Sounds exciting!" said Boneshadow as they walked back. "I've always wanted to see the palace."

Kai grinned. "Me too! But I don't think you'll be able to appear much. I'm not sure what King Godfic would say if one of his clerks turned out to be a dragon!"

# DRAGON STORM

The next day, the children gathered in the centre of the Hall. Each of them wore their official apprentice-clerk outfits – dark-grey tunics and capes – and they carried packs with clothes, feather pens, ink pots, penknives, slates and chalks; everything they would need. Malik was waiting for them, and as soon as everyone was assembled, they set off. Out of the Guild Hall, through the great doors, and along the mysterious Clockwork Corridors that led outside. Kai felt the corridors move as they walked, twisting and shuffling ahead and behind, creating an impossible maze that hid the Guild from the world.

## Kai and Boneshadow

They left through a small door in a tiny, forgotten cottage in a quiet lane. Malik checked each way, then waved the children out, and they stepped into the city of Rivven.

Rivven was the largest city in the land of Draconis. It was a sprawling, thriving place, full of merchants and craftsmen, houses

and inns, blacksmiths, tanners, carpenters, artists, and even farmers, for many small crofts and chicken coops squeezed in between the other buildings. It was dirty, smelly, loud with shouting and gossip, constantly busy, piled up on top of itself and bursting with life. Tiny passageways, great streets, smoky corners and open squares – and above them loomed the Royal Palace, sitting atop a huge hill of volcanic rock.

It was a hazy day, late summer and blue-skied, and the morning chill had already burned off. It would be hot in the city, but Malik led the children up the winding street to the palace, where the air was clear. As they reached the first gates, Kai gazed down over Rivven.

*Isn't it wonderful?* asked Boneshadow's voice in his mind, and Kai smiled.

"Yes," he murmured. Boneshadow might not be next to him, but they could stay connected and talk.

The guards waved them through into

the palace grounds, full of gardens, trees and the famous mazes that opened to the public one day every year. Malik led them to the servants' entrance around the back, and inside.

Kai was a little disappointed at first. There were kitchens, storerooms and servants' quarters that seemed quite ordinary; wood and plaster, not gold and velvet. But the rooms bustled with people dressed in white outfits or long grey suits, and the kitchens were full of steam and clattering pots and the smell of wonderful food roasting over huge fires. It was like being inside a vast and complex machine.

Malik led them to a dormitory, where they

left their things, and then brought them upstairs, past the servants and sculleries, to the west wing of the palace. Placing a finger to his lips, he opened a small door and ushered them through.

Beyond the door was a very grand room, with polished wooden floors and a high, vaulted ceiling. A large round table was placed in the middle, with three important-looking people sitting around it. Behind them were three smaller tables, overflowing with papers and books, wax and sealing stamps, and three clerks, writing frantically. The room was full of the sound of quiet talking and the scratch of pens against paper.

As the children entered, the talking

stopped and everyone turned. Kai felt suddenly very exposed, as if they'd walked into the wrong room by mistake. A man at the main table stood and strode towards them.

He looked familiar, Kai thought. He was tall, with flowing blond hair, and was well dressed in a blue suit with gold trim, leather boots and pale, fine, calfskin gloves. Malik bowed as he approached, and the children copied him.

"My lord," Malik murmured.

And suddenly Kai realised who it was.

"Hello," said Prince Harald. "Welcome to the palace."

# EXPLORING

"Thank you all for coming," said Prince Harald. "Malik tells me you're all well trained in your penmanship and clerk duties. Is that correct?"

*Among other things!* came Boneshadow's voice in Kai's mind. She sounded amused. But Kai and the others were nervous and didn't respond. Prince Harald smiled.

"Anything you can manage will help," he said. "And when our *official* clerks are feeling better, I look forward to telling them that children did their job!" He chuckled, and the children relaxed. Mira had gone rather pink, Kai realised, and Connor was gazing at the prince in admiration.

"Let me introduce you," said Prince Harald. "Here are the delegates: Lord Smale of Borolo and Captain Bright of Venn."

Lord Smale, a tall, thin, grey-robed man, gave them a slight nod and then returned to his notes. On the other side of the table, Captain Bright grinned at them. She seemed quite jolly, with rich red clothing and silver lace, and large gold earrings. She looked a little like a rich pirate.

"We've been working on this treaty for two months now and everything is nearly complete," said the prince. "You'll be helping to record the details, make copies and so on."

He smiled again. "You can see how much work there is!" The clerks at each table glanced up briefly at this, and then went back to their frantic scribbling.

Malik stepped forward and organised the children. Cara and Connor took their places behind Lord Smale, and Tom and Kai sat at the Venn table, behind Captain Bright. Erin, Mira and Ellis sat behind Prince Harald.

Kai smiled at the Venn clerk. "Hello," he said. The clerk looked up for a moment and, nodding distractedly, picked a page of writing from a stack and pushed it towards Kai.

"Three copies," she muttered.

Kai and Tom glanced at each other. Tom shrugged, and Kai took the page. He got out his ink and quill, sharpened the nib with his penknife, and started writing.

The afternoon was quite boring. The delegates argued, traded, and discussed obscure tax laws. Behind them, the clerks recorded everything they said, in triplicate. Prince Harald was the representative for Draconis and seemed quite comfortable, cheerfully smoothing arguments between the others.

Kai enjoyed clerk work, and his handwriting was reasonable. Tom, despite his large blacksmith's hands, wrote neatly and quickly, keeping up with the discussions and treaty changes. Kai glanced at the other children. Ellis and Connor were doing fine, and so was Mira, although he knew her page would be covered in ink spatters and scribbling-out, because she often daydreamed and tended to draw little designs for machines in the margins. Cara's handwriting was small and cramped, as if the letters were huddling together to keep safe. Only Erin was struggling – she didn't like clerk work, and her face was red.

At the end of the afternoon, Prince Harald clapped his hands.

"Well, my lord, my lady," he said. "I think that's a good place to pause for the day, don't you?" He beamed. "We have refreshments prepared, and entertainment for this evening."

The diplomats rose, bowed and left, and Prince Harald followed them. Malik came forward.

"Well done, all," he said. "Let's get you

fed, shall we?"

They followed him to a space near the kitchens, where the servants sat and ate. It was full of cheerful conversation and jokes, and when the children appeared the adults shuffled up on their benches and made room. Kai's hand ached from all the writing and he was covered in little splashes of ink.

After dinner, Malik returned them to their dorm in the palace and went off to finish his own work. It was still early, and upstairs they could hear music and dancing, but that was for the diplomats, and the lords and ladies.

"What do we do now?" asked Tom.

Ellis started scribbling in his notebook, mapping out the parts of the palace they'd seen so far.

"Has anyone been inside the palace before?" asked Kai.

"Once," said Cara. She didn't explain.

"I came close," said Tom. "The first time Ironskin and I flew. We chased the other dragon, the one that had started the fire, remember? It came up to the walls, and then just disappeared."

"Perhaps it returned to the dragon world?" asked Ellis, but Tom shook his head.

"There was someone on its back. It *must* have landed somewhere."

"So maybe it sneaked into the palace somehow," said Erin. "Through a secret entrance. Hey, it could still be here!"

"Maybe," said Connor, stroking his chin.

No one said anything for a few seconds. They looked at each other. And then...

"We should look for it," said Erin.

Tom grinned. "Yeah!"

"Um, are you sure?" asked Mira. "I don't know if we should be out of our rooms."

"Well, everyone thinks we're just kids," said Connor. "We can explore, and if anyone catches us we can just pretend we were playing."

Ellis looked up from his drawings. "It *would* be good to see the lower levels of the palace," he said thoughtfully.

*I'm not sure about this,* said Boneshadow's voice in Kai's head, and Kai frowned. He wasn't sure either; it seemed a risky thing to do on their very first evening. But everyone else was enthusiastic, and he didn't like to let them down, so when Tom asked him, "What do you think?", he shrugged.

"OK," he said. "Sure."

Ellis showed them his notes. "These are the levels of the palace I know about. Tom said the dragon came up to the east side, under the wall, here. So perhaps there's a way in, down these corridors?"

"Well, let's go and see," said Connor.

They crept out of the dorm. Above them, somewhere in the palace, the entertainments were still going on and the corridors were dim and empty. Cara and Ellis led, heading downwards. The corridor became darker, and felt older, and finally ended at what seemed like a solid wall.

There was no one about. Cara closed her eyes, and with a *swish* her dragon Silverthief appeared. Silverthief could spot hidden things, and now she sniffed around, then padded quietly to one brick.

"There's something strange here," she growled.

Mira came forward now and summoned her dragon, Flameteller. Flameteller also had a special ability – he could *sing* to machinery, and hear the machinery sing back. He listened, and then started to croon in a soft, silken voice, like smooth wheels turning.

A section of the wall slid open.

The children looked at each other, half nervous, half excited. The space beyond was almost pitch black and Connor lifted a burning torch from the corridor wall. By its light they could see steps leading down.

# Kai and Boneshadow

Connor stepped forward and the others followed, into the dark. Kai's heart thumped. They crept down to a wide space made of huge slabs of stone, covered in lichen. Water dripped and small stalactites hung from the ceiling. A wisp of cool air curled past them, and the scent of firewood.

Ellis looked around, making notes in his book. "I had no idea there was anything here," he murmured. "This must be nearly the oldest part of the palace. It might even be what was here *before* the palace."

"There are bars here," said Erin. Her voice sounded loud and echoey.

Kai looked ahead. She was right. Old bars, covered in rust but still strong and thick. A cage of some sort, he thought. He stepped forward and his foot scuffed against something. Reaching down, he picked up a leather pouch. It had a strange symbol on the front – a small fish on a triangle, with a crown above it. There was a heavy object inside it, like a bottle.

*The leather's dry*, said Boneshadow.

Kai frowned. Then he looked round the cavern, at the damp walls and stalactites, and realised what she meant. The pouch should be wet like everything else, but it wasn't. Why not?

*It can't have been here very long.*

"I think someone's been here recently," Kai whispered to the others, holding up the pouch. "Look!"

But then a noise came from the other side of the bars. It was a snuffling, a growling, and then a heavy *thump*, coming nearer.

Kai stared with the others. Should they run? But it was too late – the sounds were almost on them, and in the glow of Connor's burning torch he saw something stomping towards them...

A *dragon*.

# THE
# DRAGON

The dragon was twice as tall as Kai, and solidly built. It was red, with green ridges along its snout, and its eyes gleamed gold. Near the top of its neck were strange flaps of skin, like gills on a fish. They fluttered as it breathed. Its breath was a long rumble, almost like a growl.

For a moment, the children just stared. Then Kai stepped forward.

"Hello," he said, smiling. "I'm Kai."

# Kai and Boneshadow

The dragon peered at him, and then at the others. It seemed suspicious.

"It's OK," said Tom, beside Kai. "We're dragonseers. Look, this is my dragon, Ironskin."

He closed his eyes and the large, dark-red shape of Ironskin formed next to him. She bowed.

"Well met," she said. "I am Ironskin. This is my human, Tomas."

"Wait," muttered Connor. "If the dragon's here, its dragonseer must be around."

The children and their dragons looked about, worried. But then Cara said, "No – look!"

She pointed to a large chain necklace

hanging from the dragon's neck. It held a jewel pendant, glimmering green in the dim light.

"That's an emerald," she said. "Remember when we found the dragon Jadeheart? He had a jewel like that. It has

special magic, to keep a dragon in the world even when their dragonseer isn't around."

As Cara spoke, the dragon sniffed at Kai and Tom and Ironskin, and its nostrils flared. Its behaviour was strange, Kai thought. He'd met many dragons, and he liked to study them. Most were quite talkative. Closing his eyes for a moment, he concentrated and Boneshadow appeared. She studied the flaps of skin on the creature's throat.

"Are they for swimming, do you think?" she mused. "Like gills, for breathing underwater?"

Kai wasn't sure. They were quivering – in fact, the dragon's whole body was trembling.

Connor turned to Tom. "Is this the dragon you saw?"

Tom nodded. "I think so."

"Hello?" tried Connor. "Can you understand us?"

"Why is it trapped like this?" asked Mira.

Kai had a nagging feeling they were forgetting something. He glanced around the cave but there was nothing there – just ancient flagstones, blackened with soot, and plain walls. The dragon was breathing hard now, its sides moving, and through the slits in its throat Kai thought he saw a glint of something, yellow and red.

"Hoi!" bellowed Erin. She stepped forward and banged the bars. "Can you hear us, dragon?"

"Stop, you'll scare it!" said Mira. And the

creature did step back, for a moment. Then it advanced, and opened its mouth as if about to speak.

"Fire!" shouted Boneshadow suddenly. "Kai, they're for making *fire*!"

The flaps of skin opened, the dragon drew a mighty breath and Kai realised the red-yellow he could see was a flame, burning inside!

"Down!" he yelled.

"RRRRRROOAAAAAAAARRRRR!"

A blast of fire burst from the dragon's mouth!

"Arrrrrgh!" shouted the children, scrambling back. Ironskin leapt forward and closed her eyes, and the air in front of her

shimmered, stopping the flames as if they had hit a glass shield. Kai realised she was using her shielding power – but even so, he felt the heat scorch his face.

The creature stopped, and glared at them. It opened its mouth again and shrieked, so loud they had to put their hands over their ears. It was a horrible sound, full of fury, but no words.

"Stop!" tried Tom. "We're not here to hurt you!"

"Get away from it!" shouted Connor. "It's insane!"

They fled up the steps, with the creature's shriek echoing behind them. Mira's dragon Flameteller sang at the secret panel again, slamming it closed, and then the dragons faded back to their own world. The children raced back through the corridors, but Cara suddenly stopped.

"Wait!" she hissed. "Someone's coming!"

She dragged them into a hidden recess. Kai was shoved against the wall, and he heard a noise of breaking glass and felt a sharp pain in his hand.

"Ow!"

"Shh!" Cara put a finger to her lips. The children stood in shadow.

Footsteps echoed down the corridor and guards ran past. They wore black uniforms, with a silver flame embroidered on their sleeves, and they carried halberds with razor-sharp tips. Connor frowned. Cara waited a few seconds after they passed, and then nodded to the others.

Connor said, "Those weren't the usual King's Guards. Did you see their uniforms?"

"Come on," said Cara. "Before they return."

They slipped away, back to their dormitory and safety.

"Phew!" said Erin, grinning. "That was exciting!"

"*Too* exciting," said Connor. "Why did you bang on the bars like that? You scared it!"

Erin snorted. "It wasn't scared, it was

crazy! And *you* were still trying to talk to it."

A sharp pain flared in Kai's hand again, and he realised he was still holding the little leather pouch that he'd found in the cavern. A shard of green glass had poked out of it and cut a nasty gash into his palm.

*What is that?* asked Boneshadow, in his mind.

Carefully, Kai opened the pouch. Inside was a bottle, smashed, with no label. It seemed to have been full of something, but the liquid had soaked into the leather and all over his hands. It was deep blue, and it had mixed with the blood on his hand.

*You should clean that right away.* Boneshadow sounded worried, and Kai

nodded. He went to one of the bowls of water given to them for washing but, to his surprise, by the time he reached it the strange liquid had almost gone, and there was only a thin cut on his palm.

"Are you OK?" asked Mira, behind him.

"Yes," he said, peering at the cut, which

seemed hardly anything now. "I'm fine."

"So what do we do?" asked Connor.

"We should tell Malik," said Mira. "And Berin."

"We'll get into trouble," said Cara.

"Maybe." Tom shrugged. "But I've never met a dragon like that. Someone here in the palace is looking after it, feeding it... And Connor's right – those weren't normal palace guards."

"Maybe we should go back," said Kai. He suddenly felt full of energy. "Take another look, now the guards have gone?"

Everyone looked at him in surprise. "I don't know," said Mira cautiously. "Perhaps we should wait."

# Kai and Boneshadow

The others agreed. Kai shrugged. His palms were itching slightly, and he scratched at them.

"Well, let's tell Malik tomorrow and see what he says," said Tom. "We should get some sleep tonight." He grinned. "After all, it's back to more exciting clerk work tomorrow!"

Everyone groaned, but nodded, and they settled down. It took Kai a while to get to sleep; he stared into the dark for ages, still feeling that strange, wide-awake energy. When he finally drifted off, he was still scratching at his palms.

# SUSPECTS

The next day, Kai woke early. He concentrated and felt the connection open between his world and Boneshadow's.

*Good morning*, whispered Boneshadow's voice. *How's your hand?*

Kai examined his hands. His palms were still itchy, but otherwise he felt fine, and there was no sign of the cut.

"Good," he murmured. He felt wide awake, and threw off the covers and went to wash, letting the water splash and whistling loudly. Behind him, the others groaned as they woke up.

"Ugh," muttered Connor. "What time is it?"

"Time you were up, slow-bones!" called Kai. "Come on, you lazy lot!"

The others got up and ready, while Kai waited impatiently. He was keen to get on with the day, and felt again that rush of energy from last night.

"Remember, we have to tell Malik what we discovered," said Mira as they ate breakfast. But when they found Malik in the debating chamber, Prince Harald was already there.

"Good morning!" said the prince. They

bowed, but he just chuckled.

"I don't think we need to bother with that," he said. "Did you have a good evening?"

The children glanced at each other. "Yes, thank you," said Mira politely. "Very quiet."

"Nothing interesting happened at all," added Erin. Malik gave her a surprised look, but the prince didn't seem to notice anything.

"Good, good." He frowned. "Listen, there's something I need to discuss with you. Something important."

Kai swallowed. What did Prince Harald know? Had someone seen them?

"Thank you for helping with the clerk

duties," the prince said. "We appreciate it. His Majesty recognises it. The talks are at a ... tricky stage." He hesitated. "My father – the king – is concerned," he said at last. "He has heard rumours. The delegates from Borolo and Venn are here on trade talks, but they may be here for something else. The king believes ... *I* believe ... they may want to do us harm."

Kai and the others stared at him. He nodded sombrely. "You have heard the stories of dragons, right here in Rivven. We believe they may have come from outside Draconis. My father believes that foreign forces want to use dragons against us."

"My lord, are you sure?" asked Malik.
He seemed astonished. Kai almost
laughed, but then thought about it. Perhaps
this new dragon *was* from another country?
That would explain the strange uniforms of
the guards. But how could they have kept it

hidden in the king's own palace?

Prince Harald shrugged. "We are not sure. But we must keep vigilant. So, clerks: as you work today, stay alert. And if you see anything suspicious, let me know."

There was a sound at the doorway. Two servants opened the doors and the other delegates entered. Prince Harald smiled.

"Good morning!" he said cheerfully. They bowed and took their places, and the day began.

As Kai worked, he wondered about the dragon. Could it really be part of a foreign plot? Kai examined the Borolo diplomat, Lord Smale. He was tall and thin, and wore a grey padded outfit that already looked wrinkled. His face was long and pale, and his mouth moved constantly, as if he were chewing on a piece of gristle. It was easy to imagine him wanting to do harm, but hard to see him actually *doing* anything.

Kai shook his head and concentrated on his work. It was more copying, but today he found he didn't mind, and he raced through it. His pen slid smoothly over the paper, neat and fast, even better and quicker than Tom, and Kai felt a fierce joy at the idea of beating him. Then he grinned – it wasn't a competition! But if it *had* been a competition, he was winning, he thought, and grinned again.

# Kai and Boneshadow

Malik came to their dormitory after lunch to see how they were getting on, and they could finally speak to him alone. When they told him of their discovery, his face fell.

"You cannot take risks like that!" he said. "What if you'd been caught? Or hurt, even? What if someone had seen your *dragons*? You heard this morning how King Godfic fears them. What do you think he would have done?"

The children ducked their heads. "Sorry," mumbled Connor. "We thought it was important."

"And it was!" snapped Kai impatiently. Malik raised an eyebrow. "I mean, OK, we shouldn't have done it, but we found the *dragon*, Malik! Someone is keeping a dragon here in the palace!"

Malik nodded. "Yes." He rubbed his chin. "Well. This afternoon's session is the last this week, then we'll return to the Guild. Don't go exploring again, understand?"

He gave Kai a curious look and left.

The afternoon passed like the morning. The delegates made speeches and declarations, the head clerks wrote them down and the young dragonseers, as apprentice clerks, copied them out. Again, Kai found the copying easy and quick, and it was Tom who struggled to keep up.

As Kai wrote, he watched Captain Bright, the Venn diplomat who looked more like a pirate than a politician. She seemed capable of dangerous deeds, he thought – could the dragon be hers? Could she secretly be a dragonseer?

At the end of the day Prince Harald stood and thanked everyone for their progress and work. Malik led the dragonseers back through the streets of Rivven, to the old forgotten lane, and to the tiny cottage, through the hidden entrance and the winding, changing Clockwork Corridors, and into the Dragonseer Hall.

They were home.

# POWER

It was good to be back inside the Guild Hall, and Kai and the others breathed a sigh of relief. Boneshadow shimmered into view beside him and Kai rested his head against her neck.

"Hey, Bone."

"Hello, Kai," said the dragon. Her large mouth curled into a smile. "It's good to see you properly again." Then she sniffed at him. "Has something changed?"

Kai frowned. "No, why?"

"It's just..." Boneshadow tipped her head, as if confused. "There's something different about you. Are you feeling all right?"

"Yes, of course!" Kai shrugged. "I feel great!"

"How's your hand?" Kai held it out and the dragon sniffed again.

"That's strange," she said at last. "I was sure the glass had cut into the muscle."

Kai laughed. "Sorry to disappoint you!" Boneshadow was fascinated by human anatomy, just as Kai was interested in dragon anatomy, but today she just seemed to be fussing. Kai shook his head. "Really,

I'm fine. Stop worrying."

The other dragons had appeared too. Kai looked at Silverthief, who was murmuring to Cara. "Silverthief did a good job finding the hidden passage, didn't she," he remarked.

"Yes," agreed Boneshadow, still examining Kai's hand.

Kai frowned. "And Flameteller worked the secret mechanism, and Ironskin protected us from the flames." He studied Boneshadow. "You don't really *have* any powers, do you?"

Boneshadow blinked in surprise. "Well, we don't know what they'll be yet, do we? Remember what Drun taught us." She lifted her head and, in a voice surprisingly like Drun's, declared, "No one knows what a dragon's power will be, but it'll be somethin' you need, and it'll happen when you need it."

Kai chuckled. "Yeah. Wish it would hurry up though." He gazed at Boneshadow and, for the first time, had a rather unusual feeling. Boneshadow was kind, and good at caring for people. But she was a bit ... *boring*. And she was always worrying about things.

The dragon smiled at him, pleased with her impression of Drun, and Kai shook his head. What a strange thought! Boneshadow was his dragon, and he was her human, and that was all that mattered.

"Dragonseers!"

They looked up. Berin was waiting for them. For once, she wasn't smiling.

"Welcome back," she said. "Malik has told me about your adventures in the palace." She looked disapproving. "I'm sure he's already explained what a terrible risk you all took. You must not do that again, do you understand?"

They nodded. "Hmm," she said. "Well, it is done. And there is a dragon in the palace. We don't know anything about it – how it got here, whose it is, even its name. We know someone is using an emerald charm to hold it in our world. And we know that, for some reason, it is very hostile. It breathes fire. It is incredibly dangerous."

Connor said, "King Godfic thinks another country could be using dragons against us. Maybe someone from Venn or Borolo?"

Berin nodded. "His Majesty has been talking a lot about foreigners recently. He seems convinced they are a threat." She pursed her lips. "Perhaps. And yet... This must be the dragon Tomas saw months ago. Has it really been here all this time, without anyone knowing?" She sighed. "I'd rather not send you back to the palace, but that would look suspicious. You are needed for two more days, Malik tells me. So after this weekend you will return to the palace and complete your duties. *Only* your duties, mind. Let Malik know if you see anything suspicious, but do *not* go exploring again."

She gave them a stern look, but then her expression softened. "Malik says you did your work well and that Prince Harald was impressed. So go – enjoy your weekend, relax and soon we'll be done." She chuckled.

"Go! Shoo! Have fun!"

The children laughed and headed away. But as Kai and Boneshadow left, Kai glanced at Berin over his shoulder. She was talking with Malik, and she looked worried.

The next day, the dragonseers relaxed with their dragons. Ellis and Cara went off to explore more of the old ruins at the back of the huge hall. Mira, Connor and Tom were tinkering with some new invention of Mira's, and Erin had gone to Drun's hut to get help summoning her dragon, Rockhammer.

Kai wandered around with Boneshadow padding next to him. He wasn't sure what to do. He felt in a strange mood, as if he wanted to run and shout, do something energetic, but couldn't work out what. Energy fizzed inside him. His hands were itching again, wanting to move.

"Whose dragon do you think it is?" he asked. "The one in the cage?"

Boneshadow shook her long head. "I don't know. None of us recognise it. It didn't seem to want to talk. Or maybe it can't?" She blew a breath. "Berin says we should try to forget it for now."

"Hmm." That was probably sensible, Kai thought. But he wasn't feeling very sensible this morning. He nodded to Erin as she came back from Drun's hut, with Rockhammer beside her.

"Hey," she said. "Fancy another race?"

"A rematch?" asked Kai.

"A chance to catch up," she said. "If you can!"

Kai and Boneshadow exchanged glances, and Kai grinned. "We'll leave you for dust!"

# Kai and Boneshadow

They headed over to the racetrack and lined up, Kai on Boneshadow and Erin on the enormous Rockhammer.

"Ready?" asked Erin. "Steady..." Rockhammer leapt forward. "Go!" shouted Erin over her shoulder.

"Hey!" spluttered Kai. He felt a sudden, unusual surge of anger. *Cheating!* he thought. Cheating again! Well, it wouldn't help them – this time he and Boneshadow were going to win, whatever it took!

Boneshadow chased after them, Kai held on tight and inside him the fizzing energy roared.

# WINNING

They raced along the track, Rockhammer's huge legs pulling him and Erin ahead. Kai wasn't worried; the big dragon would get tired later and slow. He tucked his head down against Boneshadow's warm neck as she powered forward.

Around the first bend and into the straight. Rockhammer was still pulling ahead a little, and Kai dug his heels into Boneshadow's side.

"Ow!" she complained. "What are you doing?"

"Go faster!" he shouted. "They're getting away!"

Boneshadow grumbled but sped up, and at the second bend they were only a few metres behind. Some of the other children had stopped to watch, and behind them stood the grey-robed figure of Vice Chancellor Creedy. Kai ignored them and held on tight.

They hurtled along the next straight, and the next. Rockhammer was tiring now, and Boneshadow started to catch up. As the last turn approached, they were almost level. Rockhammer had the inside

line, Boneshadow on the outside. They could do it!

As they reached the last turn, Erin shouted something to Rockhammer. Suddenly he started drifting outwards, into Boneshadow's path! He was trying to force them into a wider turn, Kai realised. What to do? If he moved out he'd lose pace, and Erin would win. But if he kept his line, they would crash...

This was what Erin had done before, he realised. In the last race, she'd blocked them, risked them crashing, to make Kai give way. And he had, hadn't he? As the two dragons thundered on, Kai realised that he *always* gave way. He was always the one letting others win, or putting things away for them, or doing what they wanted. Always giving way, always being *nice*...

The energy fizzed inside him and he snarled, took Boneshadow's reins and *heaved* her into Rockhammer's path. Boneshadow yelped. Rockhammer was much larger, but wasn't expecting this and he reared back in shock.

"What are you doing?" gasped Boneshadow. "Let go!"

"I'm *winning*!" shouted Kai. "Now, move!"

They pulled ahead, and behind them Kai heard a *crash*. He ignored it. The air swished past and he laughed with a mad joy. Boneshadow raced along the last short straight, past the winning line and staggered to a halt.

"YASSSS!" roared Kai, punching the air. "We did it!"

He glanced about, but the other children were looking back down the track.

# Kai and Boneshadow

Turning, Kai saw Rockhammer and Erin. Rockhammer was limping, and Erin had a long scrape up one arm. For a moment Kai felt a pang of guilt. But then he remembered how they'd tried to beat him, and he grinned.

"Thought you had me at the last turn, didn't you?" he crowed.

"Are you hurt, Erin?" asked Boneshadow. She sounded concerned. "Rockhammer?"

Kai hopped off Boneshadow's back and laughed. "That's what you get for trying to cheat!" he said loudly.

Tom came forward, looking worried. "Hey, go easy," he said, giving Kai a strange look. "They had a bad fall there."

Kai shrugged. Vice Chancellor Creedy approached, and Kai looked up at him. "How was that, *sir*?" he asked, feeling pleased with himself. "Better?"

Creedy studied him. "It was certainly unlike you."

"Maybe I've just decided not to be a pushover anymore," said Kai.

"Indeed." Creedy nodded, but his eyes didn't leave Kai's, and he seemed to be thinking of something else. By now Erin and Rockhammer had reached the finishing line.

Kai grinned. "That's us even," he said. "Want a decider?"

Erin looked down at her injured arm and patted Rockhammer's side. "No," she said in a quiet voice. "Well done, Kai."

She turned and walked away.

"Kai, what's going on?" demanded Boneshadow. "That was really dangerous. Someone could have been badly hurt!"

Kai shrugged. Now the excitement of the race was over, he felt irritated. He'd beaten Erin at her own game but no one was celebrating! Even Boneshadow wasn't supporting him!

"Kai," said Tom. "Are you OK?"

# DRAGON STORM

"Of course I am!" snapped Kai. "I won, didn't I? But Erin had to make it all about her again. Just because I wouldn't let her have her way!"

Boneshadow said, "I'm worried about you—"

"Oh, shut up!" he shouted. Boneshadow stared at him in hurt astonishment. After a second she faded out of sight, back to her world.

Kai stamped away back to the dorm, ignoring the others. That was it, he thought. No more being the nice one. No more letting people take advantage of him. He was going to stand up for himself. That's what he'd done in the race.

And that's what he was going to do from now on.

Later that evening, Kai lay in his bunk, staring up at the ceiling.

Dinner had been awkward. The ones who hadn't seen the race had heard about it. Erin's arm was bandaged. Nobody talked much. It was the boys' turn to clear up, but Kai had walked away and left them to it. They owed him, he thought. How many times had he been the one left doing the work?

# DRAGON STORM

He could hear the others snoring gently, but he was wide awake. At last he crept out of the dorm and climbed up on to the roof, to a spot where the children often liked to sit, and stared out at the Hall.

It was dark. The magical globes that lit the ceiling of the Dragonseer Guild Hall were dim, like a glimmer of moonlight. Nothing was moving, no one else awake. Kai leaned against the stonework and scratched his hands.

He didn't summon Boneshadow. He didn't want her nagging him again about the race, or fussing about the cut. He hadn't told her the whole truth about that; the cut was gone but the strange itch was still there, and not just on his hands – the prickle was stretching up his arms. Like Boneshadow, Kai knew quite a lot about medicine, and at first he'd been worried it was an infection. But it was on both hands, not just the cut one, and besides, it didn't actually feel *bad*. It was quite exciting – like the tingle of being in a competition, but all the time. He felt great.

And there was something else he hadn't told Boneshadow.

He always knew when Boneshadow was around – he could feel their connection in his head. But now, as he gazed up at the darkness, he felt something else. Another creature – wilder, fiercer, more powerful.

He knew, somehow, that it was the dragon in the palace. He knew it was a he, and that he wanted to get out of his cage. He knew he wanted to breathe fire again. He was dangerous, and exciting! And somehow, Kai was now connected to him...

Kai sat on the roof of the dorm, watched the darkness, and smiled.

# BACK AT
# THE PALACE

The next morning, Kai woke up and thought about his strange dream. But ... *had* it been a dream? Or had he really sat on the dorm roof in the middle of the night? Had he really felt another dragon out there? The *palace* dragon?

He shook his head and opened the connection to Boneshadow.

"Hey," he murmured. Boneshadow didn't reply. Kai suddenly remembered how he'd behaved the previous day, and felt embarrassed and shocked. What had got into him?

"Sorry, Bone," he whispered. "I shouldn't have shouted like that. I don't know what happened. I'll say sorry to Erin and Rockhammer too, I promise."

Now he felt that whisper in his mind, and Boneshadow's happy voice.

*Thank you. I'm a bit worried about you, Kai.*

Kai sighed.

"I'm fine, really." He felt weirdly reluctant to talk about the itching in his arms – now up to his shoulders, he realised. Besides, he really *did* feel good. He was full of energy, and the world seemed sharper, somehow. There was no reason to worry.

At breakfast he made an effort to smooth things with the others. Everyone seemed happy to forgive him, even Erin.

"Oh, it's just a scratch," she said, lifting her bandaged arm. "And Rocky's leg is OK too." She grinned. "We'll have that decider

sometime soon, yeah?"

Kai smiled in relief. "Sure."

They had a relaxing day, taking it easy and getting ready for their trip back to the palace. A few times Kai looked up at the cavern roof, trying to recall the sense of the other dragon out there, but there was nothing.

But the following day, as soon as Kai stepped through the servant doors and into the palace, he felt the connection again, so strong and clear that he gasped.

*Kai, are you all right?* asked Boneshadow's voice. Kai didn't know how to answer. He nodded vaguely, feeling the presence in his mind. It *was* the other dragon! He could feel his strength and rage. And a name...

*Firedreamer*.

None of the other children seemed to have noticed anything. Kai wondered if he should say something, but a strange instinct told him to keep quiet. He knew something they didn't, he thought. That was a kind of ... power.

Shaking his head, he followed the others to their dorm.

*Firedreamer*, he wondered. *What's your story?*

Malik brought them to the debating chamber and they took their places. Again, Kai found he was racing through the work, better than he'd ever managed before, and even the head clerk seemed impressed. It was easy – he hardly even had to concentrate. He watched the foreign diplomats as they argued over the treaty. Could they be the enemy? Could they be the ones who had brought Firedreamer into the palace?

The day went quickly, and Malik was pleased. The last few details had been sorted; there would be a celebration feast this evening to mark the treaty, and an official signing tomorrow morning, and then they would be done.

"I'm afraid lowly clerks are not invited to the feast," he said, smiling wryly. "Only the lords and ladies. But I'll make sure the chef sends some of the food your way."

# Kai and Boneshadow

The others cheered, but Kai felt suddenly angry. *Why* weren't they invited? They'd done all the work! Other people were taking advantage of him, again! But he didn't say anything. Instead, he forced a smile and kept his anger hidden.

"So what shall we do?" asked Erin.

Connor brought out a bag of dice. "Fancy a game?"

There was a groan from everyone; Connor was excellent at dice, and almost always won. Although, this evening Kai thought he would have a chance. He felt sharp, full of fire, three steps ahead of everyone, as if his anger was a kind of energy. The itching sensation had spread across his shoulders, even to his chest. He felt like he wanted to run, or shout, or fight something...

"We should go back to the dragon," he said.

The others turned in astonishment. "What? No!" said Mira. "Didn't you hear what Berin said?"

"But this is our last chance!" said Kai. "After the signing, we'll be sent home. Don't you want to find out what's going on?"

Tom shook his head. "Kai, we can't."

*We can't do that, Kai*, said Boneshadow. *Berin said not to*.

Kai shook his head. "I can't believe you lot," he said. "We've got a chance to learn something *important* and you're all huddled here like ... like cowards!"

Erin bristled. "Hey, I'm not a coward!"

"Kai, what's happening?" asked Tom, looking concerned. "You seem really different. Are you feeling all right?"

Kai stood. "I'm sick of people asking that!" he snapped. "And I'm sick of always doing what I'm told! I'm going, with or without you!"

He stormed out of the room before anyone could react, and slipped down the corridor.

*Kai, what are you doing?!* came Boneshadow's voice. *This is wrong! We have to go back!*

"Oh, *stop*!" snarled Kai. "You're just

like the others, telling me what to do!"

*That's not what I mean—* started Boneshadow, but Kai shook his head.

"You know what?" he hissed. "I don't think you're even my real dragon. All you do is nag. And you can't do *anything*.

"Firedreamer can breathe flames, did you see that? That's *real* power!"

*What? Who's Firedreamer? Kai, listen to me—*

"No."

He broke the connection, and Boneshadow's voice disappeared.

Kai grinned. Enough of old Bone! He was going to get a *real* dragon. He moved silently, quickly, scratching at his neck and

# Kai and Boneshadow

the itch that had now reached his head.

# FIRE-
# DREAMER

Kai slipped down the corridors, towards the call of the dragon Firedreamer.

The dragon's connection was clear in his mind now; a raw, burning power so very different to Boneshadow's. It made Kai want to laugh with delight, but he kept silent, sneaking noiselessly through the corridors.

He stopped at a corner and peered round, and saw a squad of the King's Guards standing to attention. Captain Hork, the head of the King's Guards, was there too, in a shining helmet with a ridiculously tall plume. He was shouting at the others because their breastplates weren't polished highly enough.

Kai sniggered. How different Hork was to the guards that had chased them before! How pathetic! He retraced his steps and took a different route. It was easy; he felt as if he had the map of the palace in his mind. Everything was simple now.

He reached the place Cara had found, and the wall with the hidden entrance. Before, they'd needed Silverthief and Flameteller to find and work the mechanism, but within a minute of searching, Kai found the latch that held the entrance closed. The wall slid open and dank air flowed out. Kai entered. It was still dark, but he could make out the edges of walls and the steps, and he could remember the route they'd taken before. Down the steps, into the room that was so old it was almost a cave...

The dragon lurked in the darkness, snuffling and growling. Kai stood at the bars of his cage and smiled.

"Come forward," he said. "Come forward, Firedreamer."

And slowly, cautiously, Firedreamer approached. He stopped at the bars and sniffed the air, and glared at Kai. His air slits trembled and he drew in a breath...

# Kai and Boneshadow

"Stop!" commanded Kai. "You won't harm me."

The creature trembled and then blew the breath out again. He bowed his head.

Kai grinned. He felt *amazing*. The itch was all through his body now, like bottled lightning, ready to strike. He felt invincible. And Firedreamer was *his* dragon now. Not just a companion, but actually *under his control*. Kai stepped up to the bars. There was a bolt by his side, and he undid it.

"Kai!"

Kai turned. Tom was on the steps, holding a burning torch.

"I came to find you," he said. He looked at the bolt, alarmed. "Kai, what are you doing?

Don't let it out!"

He rushed down the last steps and faced Kai. A second later, Ironskin appeared. She stood between them and Firedreamer, ready to provide a shield.

Kai smiled. "It's OK, Tom. This is my new dragon. His name is Firedreamer."

"Kai, listen to me," said Tom. "It's the liquid – the stuff you got on your hands, remember?"

Kai frowned. "What?"

"That's what Connor thinks," said Tom. "He says it soaked into you – it's affecting you. It's *changing* you. Can't you feel it?"

Kai held his hands up. There was nothing there. Just that strange, powerful itch.

"Something's very wrong, Kai!" said Tom.

Kai stared at Tom and nodded.

"Yes," he said at last. "Yes. There *is* something wrong. It's *you*. You're trying to tell me what to do, again. Just like everyone else, thinking you can order me around. Thinking I'll be *nice*. Well, that's changed."

Kai swung open the cage door.

"No!" shouted Tom.

Firedreamer padded forward, and Ironskin and Tom stepped back. Tom said, "Stay behind Ironskin, Kai!"

Kai laughed. "He's no danger, are you, Firedreamer? Not to *me*, anyway..."

The dragon turned his head towards Tom, and then at Ironskin. His nostrils flared as he breathed in.

"Watch out!" shouted Ironskin.

Firedreamer roared! A blast of flame bounced off Ironskin's shield.

"We have to get out of here!" shouted Tom.

Ironskin tried to back up the steps with Tom, but Firedreamer came forward again and blasted another fiery breath. Ironskin was forced to stop and form her shield again. The two dragons squared off against each other, their long necks moving, their teeth bared.

Kai stood to one side, grinning. Firedreamer was so powerful! It was exciting! And yet... As he watched, he

had a strange feeling, as if this was all happening to someone else. It was wonderful, hearing Firedreamer's roar. It was funny seeing Ironskin trying to defend herself! But all the time, he felt he could hear someone shouting at him. Shouting that something was wrong...

Firedreamer leapt forward again, and Ironskin and Tom staggered back.

"This isn't you, Kai!" gasped Tom.

"Maybe it's me now!" shouted Kai. "I'm tired of being *nice*! I'm tired of you telling me what to do!"

"I'm not!" shouted Tom. "You're my friend, Kai! Please! We're trying to *help*!"

Kai scowled. No. No, that wasn't right.

# Kai and Boneshadow

He was better now, more powerful, sharper, smarter – he didn't need any help! And now he had a powerful dragon, one he could control! But... He shook his head. The voice was calling to him. He held his hands up again and looked at them. Could there be something wrong? Something inside him ... *changing* him?

*Yes!* said the voice. *Listen to us, Kai!*

"Boneshadow?" murmured Kai.

Firedreamer shrieked and drove forward. As Ironskin reared to defend herself, Firedreamer swung his huge tail round, smashing into Tom's legs. There was a horrible *crack*, and Tom yelped in pain and collapsed.

"Tomas!" cried Ironskin. Tom had fainted, and her connection to him was lost, and she was fading. "Tomas!"

And then she was gone.

Firedreamer roared in triumph and stomped towards Tom's body.

Kai frowned. "Tom?" he asked. This was

wrong. Something was *wrong*. "Tom?"

*Tom's in danger, Kai!*

Firedreamer stood over Tom, snarling, and lifted one huge paw above his head.

"Tom?"

Kai stared at Tom, and just for a moment the strange fog in his mind seemed to part. Suddenly he realised what was happening.

"Wait!" he shouted, running forward. "Stop! *Tom!*"

The paw came slamming down.

# POWER

"STOP!" shouted Kai, rushing forward. "Move away!"

Firedreamer, his paw centimetres from Tom's head, glared at Kai. His golden eyes were fierce and wild. Beneath him, Tom lay unconscious, one leg bent at a terrible angle.

"Oh, Tom!" gasped Kai. "What have I done?"

The dragon lifted his paw again.

"NO!" bellowed Kai. He raised a hand.

"Stop, I *order* you!"

He could still feel the energy through his body, the strange itch in his blood. He could feel Firedreamer and his frustrated fury, and the power Kai had over him. He was fighting to break free – the sides of his chest trembled as he breathed, the air slits shivered and the fire inside his throat flared, ready to roar.

"*No*," he demanded again, with all his will. "*Not my friend!*"

Firedreamer hesitated, and then his head dipped and he stepped away.

"Back!" ordered Kai. "Back in the cage!"

Slowly, fighting every step, the dragon walked back into the cage. Kai slammed the bolt closed with shaking hands, and raced

back to Tom. What was he going to do? He needed help.

"Bone?" he whispered.

Boneshadow appeared almost immediately. "I'm here, Kai."

Kai felt a wave of relief at seeing her. "Tom needs help!" he said. "He's hurt, Bone, and it's my fault. It's my fault!"

Boneshadow padded across to Tom and sniffed at his leg. She was bristling, her shoulders hunched, and Kai suddenly remembered everything he'd said over the last few days. He lifted his hand to his mouth in horror.

"Bone, I'm so sorry! I don't know what's happening!"

# DRAGON STORM

Boneshadow turned and scowled at him for a long time, her face fierce and grim.

Then, finally, she smiled.

"Kai, you're my human, and I'm your dragon. Whatever's happening, we'll face it together."

Kai let out a shaky breath. "Oh, thank you!" He wrapped his arms around her neck. "I'm sorry!"

"We have to help Tomas," said Boneshadow. Kai nodded and examined his friend's leg. He knew about dragon anatomy, and had to hope humans were similar.

"It's his tibia, I think – his shin bone. I think it's shattered." There was a lot of blood. Kai bit his lip. "We could try to carry him, but that could make it worse."

"Kai..." murmured Boneshadow.

Kai closed his eyes. Even now, the power inside him was whispering again, telling him to leave Tom, dismiss Boneshadow, release Firedreamer. It was a power that wanted to destroy. He pushed it down.

"I'll have to get help," he muttered.

"Kai, wait."

Kai turned. Boneshadow was trembling. She lifted her head. "Kai, I think it's happening. I think this is my power."

"What? Really?"

Boneshadow nodded. Her back arched. "Keep Tomas steady," she whispered. "Hold his leg."

She lowered her head and peered at the wound. "Yes," she murmured. Softly, she breathed out...

Kai gasped. Beneath his hands he felt the broken bone in Tom's leg moving! "Are you doing that?" he asked in astonishment.

# Kai and Boneshadow

Boneshadow breathed again. Now the pieces were reassembling, as if the break was happening in reverse. As Kai stared, the leg straightened and lost its dreadful loose feeling, and the skin healed. Soon he could feel the bone, whole again.

"That's incredible," he murmured. "Boneshadow, you can *heal*!" He remembered complaining about her not having powers, and felt ashamed. "You have the best power of all."

Boneshadow nodded and looked up at him. "Now you," she said.

Kai blinked. "What?" Then he realised what she meant. The itching was still there. He was holding it back for now, but it would return, he could feel it. For a moment, he was angry again. He didn't want to lose this power! Boneshadow wanted to take it from him! But he ground his teeth together and stood. This was poison. It wasn't him.

"All right," he whispered.

Boneshadow stood in front of him and breathed her soft breath.

It felt *awful*. As Boneshadow's breath surrounded him, the itch flared up all over his body, so that he wanted to scratch forever. It roared in his head and chest, and then his shoulders. Gradually it moved back down to his arms, down to just his hands, and then the tips of his fingers, like pins and needles.

And then it was gone. Kai let out a

shuddering sob and almost fell over. He felt empty and weak. But gradually his strength came back. And with it, he realised just how wrong the power had felt before. He was himself again, in his own body. It was like coming back home after staying somewhere horrible.

"Thank you," he said.

He reached down and shook Tom's shoulder gently. "Tom?"

Tom muttered something and shivered. Then his eyes opened wide and he stared at Kai. "The dragon!" he shouted. He looked at Kai in astonishment, and then around him, and at the cage, barred again. Slowly his gaze returned to Kai.

"What happened?" he asked. "I thought my leg was hurt."

"Boneshadow healed you," said Kai.

Tom examined Kai. "What about you?" he asked cautiously.

"I'm fine," said Kai. "A bit tired, but back to normal. You saved me." He smiled. "And Boneshadow healed me too." He looked around. Firedreamer was still locked in the cage, growling. But as their eyes met, the dragon seemed to realise that Kai's connection with him was gone. His nostrils flared, and he padded forward again...

"We need to go," said Kai.

Leaning on each other, they staggered up the steps and out of the cave.

# HEART-BANE

The signing ceremony was very grand. It took place in the Royal Banquet Hall, in front of the king himself. King Godfic gave a short speech, during which he glared at the diplomats from Borolo and Venn as if trying to decide whether to haul them off to the dungeons. Prince Harald spoke next, thanking everyone and wishing them a safe journey home.

The dragonseers watched from a corner

of the Hall, where Malik had sneaked them in. It was a great honour, but Kai didn't pay much attention. He concentrated on making himself as inconspicuous as possible, and didn't look anyone in the face.

He'd told the others the full story. Afterwards, they'd said they were pleased he was better and glad no one had been seriously hurt. But they were cautious, and Kai still felt dreadful at what had nearly happened, and what he'd done.

After the signing, Malik brought them back home and Kai asked to speak to Berin. In her office, he told her what had happened. Berin didn't interrupt, or ask any questions. She listened, her face calm, and then asked

# Kai and Boneshadow

Kai to wait in the next room.

He waited a long time. Boneshadow kept him company, chatting about the signing ceremony, and how nice it was to be back home, and her new powers, and wondering what they would be doing next. Kai knew she was just making conversation to keep him distracted, but it was nice.

At last Berin asked him back through to her office. When he entered, Vice Chancellor Creedy was there, and Malik too. They looked grim.

"Show me your hands," barked Creedy. Kai blinked and held them out. Creedy brought out a small blue stone from his robes and passed it over Kai's fingers,

one by one, and then examined it.

"Heartbane," he said at last. "As we suspected."

Berin sighed. "I wish you had told us, Kai. We could have helped."

"I didn't really know what was happening," said Kai. "I still don't."

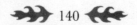

# Kai and Boneshadow

"The vial of liquid you found is called heartbane," said Berin. "A powerful and dangerous potion. It is banned almost everywhere. It makes you stronger, faster, sharper... But it is a destructive power. It harms your soul."

"When the vial smashed, the potion was absorbed into your skin," said Creedy. "Foolish boy to not tell us. Did you think the way it disappeared was normal?"

Kai shook his head. "I'm sorry," he said. "I know I'll have to leave."

Berin frowned. "Leave?"

"Well, yes," said Kai, surprised. "I mean – I hurt Erin and Rockhammer. I broke the rules. I almost got Tom killed!"

Berin nodded. "Hmm. Well, I think we can assume you weren't in full control. Mr Creedy?"

Creedy scowled. "According to the old texts, a dose of heartbane – a *strong*, dangerous dose – is approximately three drops."

"Three drops," said Berin. "That's a dangerous amount. You had the whole vial. It should have driven you wild. It should have burned you up, turned you into a monster."

"It did," whispered Kai.

"It did *not*," replied Berin firmly. "Something in you fought it all the way. You held it off for days, and even when it finally took you over, you freed yourself from it when Tomas became hurt."

"That was Boneshadow," said Kai. "She called to me. She was the one who woke me up."

"And how did Boneshadow reach you?" asked Berin. "A dragon cannot make the connection. *You* must have done it, without knowing. When things were at their worst, somehow you reached for help. It was the best thing you could possibly do." She smiled. "Kai, you are a good person. The others will forgive you, because none of this *was* you. Now, tell me – can you still feel this other dragon, this Firedreamer?"

Kai tried, but he already knew the answer.

He'd been trying since last night.

"No."

"Heartbane has another use," said Creedy. "When combined with certain magic, the old books say it can give you power to control a dragon."

"Someone at the palace is holding him a prisoner," said Berin. "They are using an emerald charm to prevent him from returning to the dragon world, and heartbane to control him."

"It's monstrous," said Malik. He looked furious.

"Indeed," said Berin. "And very dangerous. Tell me, Kai, is there anything you saw that might help us identify who is doing this?"

Kai thought. "King Godfic thinks it's someone from Venn or Borolo," he said.

Berin pursed her lips. "Perhaps."

"Oh, there was a crest!" said Kai, suddenly remembering. "On the leather pouch. It looked like a fish, I think. Can I have a piece of paper?" Berin passed one across and Kai drew the shape, as well as he remembered it – a small fish on a triangle, with a crown above it.

"Does that help?"

Berin studied it

and glanced at Creedy.

"Yes," she said carefully. "Thank you, Kai. I think we need to consider this." She smiled again. "Well. You may return to the others."

Kai left, and Boneshadow appeared again. She leaned her head against his.

"Poor Firedreamer," said Kai. "I wish I'd taken the emerald pendant off him. Imagine being held like that, not even able to go back to your own world. Do you think that's why he's so wild?"

"Perhaps," murmured Boneshadow. "There's something very wrong. The way he is in this world doesn't feel right." She shook her head.

They walked towards the hut where

the dragonseers ate. Kai hesitated as they reached the door.

"It's all right, Kai," said Boneshadow. She faded out of sight, but he could still feel their connection. *I'm here with you.*

Kai smiled and nodded, and entered the hut. Everyone was there, chattering, but when Kai entered, they stopped and gazed at him. He blushed.

"Um," he said. "Look, I just... I wanted to say I'm sorry—"

"Budge up," said Tom.

Kai stopped. "What?"

"Not you, her," said Tom, and poked Erin. "Budge up and make a space."

Erin shuffled along. She grinned at Kai.

"Better be quick. Hilda's made pies and I've already had three." She scooped up another one. "Make that four," she said through a mouthful.

"So..." Kai hesitated. "So, it's OK?"

"Don't be silly," said Connor. "We figured it out. Something in the potion made you an idiot. Now you're better."

Mira smiled at him. "Everyone knows you're the nicest out of all of us," she said. "That's how we knew there was something wrong."

Kai looked at them all. "Thank you," he said shyly. "I just—"

"Oh, sit down!" ordered Erin. Kai sat next to her and she thumped him on the back

so hard he almost tipped into a bowl of
mashed potatoes. "Eat; get your strength
up. Because tomorrow I'm going to *crush*
you in another race."

Kai smiled. "Maybe." He wondered,
though. It was wonderful to be back
to normal, but ... perhaps he had been
a bit of a pushover before? It had felt

good to win! Perhaps next time he'd give Erin a surprise…

"Maybe," he said again and, grinning, he picked up one of Hilda's famous pastry pies. "Or maybe not!"

# EPILOGUE

"Connor," asked Kai after dinner. "Have you ever seen this before?"

He drew the shape he'd seen on the leather pouch. Connor peered at it. "Hmm, looks familiar. What's it from?"

"It was on the pouch," said Kai. "Berin thinks whoever owns the pouch is the one holding Firedreamer."

Connor fetched an old book and thumbed through it. "Here," he said, pleased. "It's something called ... the Seal of Culon."

He read the article. "It says Culon was the first King of Draconis after the Dragon Storm. This was his personal seal. It's been

passed down to his descendants ever since." He stopped reading. "Wait, this can't be right."

"Descendants?" asked Mira.

Kai frowned. "But that means..."

"That means it was the *king's* pouch," said Cara. "King Godfic's pouch."

"It's the king," said Kai. "It's been the king, all along."

*"King Godfic is the dragonseer!"*